BOOK ANALYSIS

By Georgina Murphy

A Thousand Splendid Suns

BY KHALED HOSSEINI

BrightSummaries.com

KHALED HOSSEINI

AFGHAN-BORN AMERICAN WRITER

- **Born in Kabul, Afghanistan, in 1965.**
- **Notable works:**
  - *The Kite Runner* (2003), best-selling novel
  - *And The Mountains Echoed* (2014), novel
  - *Sea Prayer* (2018), illustrated short story

Khaled Hosseini was born in Kabul, but his family fled Afghanistan for America in 1978 after the Soviet invasion. Whilst in America, Hosseini obtained a medical degree and began writing alongside his work in 2001. *The Kite Runner* was Hosseini's first novel, for which he was awarded the Boeke Prize and the Alex Award, amongst others. His next novel, *A Thousand Splendid Suns* (2007) was a *New York Times* best seller for 103 weeks, whilst *And The Mountains Echoed* (2013) similarly appeared as number one on the *Times* list. His novels are all partly set in Afghanistan, and give voice to Afghan protagonists. Hosseini's novels have been described as the "saddest of stories" (Memmott, 2004:

para. 13), whereby he intertwines painful and compelling narratives with accurate historical events, stressing the effects of large-scale conflict and international politics on individual lives.

A THOUSAND SPLENDID SUNS

HISTORICAL FICTION

- **Genre:** novel
- **Reference edition:** Hosseini, K. (2007) *A Thousand Splendid Suns*. London: Bloomsbury.
- **1st edition:** 2007
- **Themes:** love, pain, conflict, history, war, marriage, violence, mother-daughter love, sacrifice

Within *A Thousand Splendid Suns*, Hosseini focuses on the lives of two women, Mariam and Laila. The first section of the novel takes us through Mariam's youth and her marriage at just 15 years old to a man named Rasheed. In part two, Hosseini turns to Laila's youth nearly two decades later. When Laila's family are all killed in the war, she is taken in and cared for by Mariam and Rasheed. As Laila later marries Rasheed, the lives of Mariam and Laila intertwine and they develop a bond as close as that of mother and daughter. Whilst *The Kite Runner* is a "father and son story set exclusively in the world of men", with *A Thousand Splendid Suns,* Hosseini sought to tell the "inner lives of two struggling Afghan women" (Hosseini, 2007: 409): as they endure the conflict within their domestic lives as well as the war around them, Hosseini demonstrates how mother-daughter bonds move both women to acts of complete selflessness.

SUMMARY

MARIAM'S CHILDHOOD

The first part of the novel focuses on Mariam's childhood. When she is five years old, her mother calls her a "harami" (p. 3), which means an illegitimate child. Mariam's father Jalil visits her for one to two hours every Thursday, and is always full of affection for Mariam and gives her lots of presents. We then learn that Jalil has "three wives and [...] nine legitimate children" (p. 5), and owns a cinema, as well as land and other stores. Nana (Mariam's mother) used to work for Jalil as a housekeeper, until they had an affair and Nana fell pregnant; she was subsequently thrown out of the house. We are introduced to Mullah Faizullah, who teaches Mariam parts of the Koran: when Mariam and Mullah Faizullah ask Nana if she can go to school, Nana refuses and tells Mariam that she must only learn to "endure" (p. 18).

In "the spring of 1974" (p. 25), Mariam turns 15. Mariam asks her father if she can go and see a new cartoon that is on in Jalil's cinema, but he becomes uncomfortable and refuses. Away from Nana, Mariam asks him again, and this time he tells her to meet him outside the house tomorrow. When Nana learns of Mariam and Jalil's plan, she calls Mariam ungrateful and says she will "die if you go" (p. 27). On her birthday, Mariam waits outside for Jalil, who does not arrive, so she decides to walk to Herat instead. When she is not allowed to enter her father's house, she spends the night outside. She later sees her father watching her from the window but he still refuses her entry. When Mariam gets home, she finds that Nana has hanged herself. Mariam then goes to live with her father, who arranges for her to marry a man named Rasheed. We learn that Rasheed's first wife and son have both died. They marry the next day.

MARIAM'S MISERABLE MARRIAGE

For the first few days of her marriage to Rasheed, Mariam stays cooped up in her room in fear of her husband. After a few days, he orders her to "start behaving like a wife" (p. 63). Rasheed gives her a burqa to wear when she leaves the house, and also buys her a silk shawl that Mariam regards as a "true gift" compared to her father's "halfhearted tokens of penance" (p. 75). That night, Mariam and Rasheed have sex. One day, Mariam searches Rasheed's room and finds a gun, pornographic magazines, and pictures of his wife and son. Mariam falls pregnant and they organise a party in celebration; however, before they get the chance to celebrate, Mariam has a miscarriage.

In 1978, Mariam turns 19, and the reader learns that she has gone through six pregnancies, all of which have ended with a miscarriage. Rasheed turns cruel, hating Mariam because she has not given him a baby boy. The first part of the novel ends with Rasheed complaining about the rice that Mariam has apparently overcooked. He then forces a handful of pebbles into her mouth and forces her to chew, claiming, "now you know what your rice tastes like" (p. 103).

LAILA'S CHILDHOOD

The narrative shifts to Laila's story, beginning in Kabul in the spring of 1978. Laila is nine years old. We learn that her best friend Tariq is away for a

13-day trip with his parents, meaning that Laila is very grumpy because she misses him. After 13 days, Tariq does not come back, and it is a few weeks before he returns. Laila's family are informed that Laila's brothers, Ahmad and Noor, have died in the war. Laila's mother is distraught and refuses to leave her bed. One night when Laila goes into her mother's room, she admits to Laila "I haven't been much of a mother to you" (p. 141).

In April 1988, Laila's father comes home with the news that the Soviets are withdrawing from Afghanistan, but are leaving a "puppet president" (p. 151) in place. The narrative then jumps forward from January 1989, when the last of the Soviet forces leave Kabul, to 1992, when the Soviet Union "crumbled with astonishing swiftness" (p. 157). In Kabul, the Soviet puppet government falls to the Mujahideen rebels, and the whole town celebrates. That night, Laila and Tariq go to the same party, and she gets jealous of the attention he is receiving from other girls. They sneak out of the party to a more private area, but then witness a violent fight between different ethnic groups. Hosseini makes it clear that these tensions reflect the political climate within the Mujahideen, different subsets of which are preparing for war with each other: "the Mujahideen, armed to the teeth but now lacking a common enemy, had now found the enemy in each other" (p. 169).

War breaks out, putting innocent civilians like Laila in danger. She does not go anywhere without Tariq. One day, Tariq tells Laila that he has bought a gun so that he will be able to protect her. The two then share their first kiss. In August 1992, Tariq tells Laila he is leaving to go to Pakistan with his family. Laila is distraught, and knowing that they may never see each other again, they have sex. Tariq then asks Laila to marry her, but she cannot bring herself to leave her father. Tariq promises that he will come back for her. A few weeks later, Laila's family decide to leave Afghanistan; however, as they are packing up the car, a rocket hits the house and Laila's parents are killed. The second part of the novel ends with Laila's faint awareness that she is being cared for by two people.

TWO NARRATIVES COMBINE

The reader learns it is Mariam and Rasheed who nurse Laila back to health, having found her stuck under the rubble. Miraculously, Laila manages to escape with "relatively minor injuries" (p. 195). One day, a man named Abdul Sharif visits Laila to inform her that Tariq died in an intensive care unit in Pakistan. Laila continues to stay at Rasheed's house, and Mariam soon realises that he means to marry her. Laila instantly agrees, and the reader realises it is because she is pregnant with Tariq's child. They marry soon after. Laila's marriage to Rasheed is a source of tension between the two women, as Mariam accuses Laila of stealing her husband. In the spring of 1993, Laila gives birth to a baby girl named Aziza. The birth of a girl causes Rasheed and Laila to fight continuously, and one night Mariam finds Laila and Aziza sleeping on the floor downstairs. As Aziza awakes, Mariam plays with her for the first time. A few days later, Mariam leaves a pile of baby clothes for Laila outside her room, and the two women soon bond over a cup of chai tea.

Mariam and Laila develop a mother-daughter relationship and begin to share their stories with one another. Laila tells Mariam that she plans to escape to Pakistan with Aziza, and asks Mariam to accompany them. However, on the day of their escape they are caught by the police and forced back to Rasheed, who beats Mariam and locks Laila and Aziza in a room without food or drink. The narrative then jumps to September 1996, when Afghanistan has been taken over by the Taliban. Although the fighting has stopped, the Taliban has implemented highly restrictive laws on society. Laila then falls pregnant with Rasheed's child, and nine months later undergoes an emergency Caesarean section to give birth to a baby boy named Zalmai.

In the year 2000, Kabul is in the midst of a three-year drought, and that summer Rasheed's shop burns to the ground. They become desperate for money, and the following year are forced to send Aziza to an orphanage because they cannot afford to care for her. One day, Rasheed agrees to take Laila, Mariam and Zalmai to the orphanage, and on their return Laila sees Tariq standing outside her door. When Laila and Tariq talk, we find out that he went to a refugee camp in Pakistan after escaping Kabul, where his father died and his mother became very ill. In an attempt to get money, Tariq agreed to a drug-smuggling operation, but was caught and sent to prison for seven years. Laila tells Tariq about Aziza. That night, Zalmai ignorantly tells Rasheed about Tariq's visit, and he begins to strangle Laila. Fearing that he means to kill her, Mariam hits Rasheed in the temple with a shovel and he dies. The next morning, Mariam tells Laila that she must leave Kabul with Tariq and her children, while Mariam will take the punishment. Mariam is sent to prison and soon after executed.

LAILA'S HAPPY MARRIAGE

Having escaped Kabul, Laila and Tariq marry and live in Murree. They soon learn that, following 9/11, the United States has declared war on Afghanistan. The narrative then jumps to 2002, when Afghanistan is beginning to stabilize. Subsequently, Laila tells Tariq that she wishes to return to Kabul. Prior to this, however, Laila wishes to pass through Mariam's hometown, Herat. Whilst there, she meets Mariam's tutor's son Hamza, who tells her that Mullah Faizullah has passed away. They then visit Mariam's old house, and afterwards Hamza gives Laila a tin box that Jalil hoped would be passed to Mariam at some point. Inside the box is a copy of Pinocchio, a letter of apology to Mariam from Jalil, and Mariam's inheritance. Back in Kabul, Laila uses this money to fund the orphanage. The novel ends with Laila's realisation that she is pregnant with another child, and her affirmation that if it is a girl, she will be named after Mariam.

CHARACTER STUDY

MARIAM

Mariam was born in Herat in 1959, and the first thing the reader learns about her is that she is an illegitimate child. Her mother calls her "a clumsy little *harami*" (p. 4). Hosseini makes it clear that whilst at five years old she does not understand what this means, in adulthood she realises its significance, for as an "illegitimate person" she "would never have legitimate claim to the things other people had, such as love, family, home, acceptance" (*ibid.*). As such, in the first part of the novel Mariam is treated with little love by her father. For example, when she visits Jalil at his house in Herat, he first pretends that he is not in and then refuses her entry:

> "The face was there for an instant, a flash, but long enough. Long enough for Mariam to see the eyes widen, the mouth open. Then it snapped away from view. A hand appeared and frantically pulled at a cord. The curtains fell shut." (p. 34)

This episode signals Jalil's panic at the fact that Mariam has seen him within the house even though he is pretending that he is not in. However, the way "the curtains fell shut" literally reflects how he closes the door on Mariam, and thus denies her the unconditional, unashamed parental love he gives to his other children. During her childhood, Mariam is thus plagued by her father's adultery – "she was the walking, breathing embodiment of their shame" (p. 48) – and such disgrace follows her into married life. Rasheed alienates her as a "*harami*" who "grew up in a *kolba* made of mud *outside* the village" (p. 216), whereby Hosseini's italicisation of the word "outside" emphasises the fact that Mariam is a social outcast. As such, in the first part of the novel, Mariam's future seems rather bleak: she is trapped in an unhappy and childless marriage, but unable to escape Rasheed's control.

However, once Mariam meets Laila, her hopes for the future begin to change. Despite initially hating Laila for "steal[ing] [her] husband" (p. 219), the birth of Aziza brings the two women close. Mariam becomes "eager for the three cups of *chai* she and Laila would share in the yard", and gets "anxious" if "Laila and Aziza [sleep] in" (p. 245). The bond between Laila and Mariam develops into something of a mother-daughter relationship, whereby the two women protect each other from Rasheed's violence:

> "Then an astonishing thing happened: [Laila] lunged at him. She grabbed his arm with both hands and tried to drag him down, but she could do no more than dangle from it. She did succeed in slowing Rasheed's progress toward Mariam." (p. 235)

As Laila puts herself in danger in order to stop Rasheed attacking Mariam, it becomes clear that their concern for one another is stronger than their desire for individual self-preservation. Furthermore, Mariam later gratefully tells Laila "nobody's ever stood up for me before" (p. 243), signifying how unique and special their bond is to her. Mariam returns this notion of protection for Laila later on in the novel: when it becomes clear that Rasheed means to strangle Laila to death, Mariam kills Rasheed: she "brought down the shovel. This time, she gave it everything she had" (p. 341). In their desire to protect one another, both women give each other strength against Rasheed's violence. Furthermore, by encouraging Laila to escape following Rasheed's death, Mariam sacrifices herself in order to save those that have effectively become her family. In their final conversation, Mariam tells Laila "everything I'd ever wished for as a little girl you've already given me. You and your children have made me so very happy" (p. 350). Mariam therefore becomes a heroic, self-sacrificing figure.

LAILA

When we first meet Laila, it is immediately apparent that she will grow up to be a woman of a modern and more forward-thinking society. She was born in 1978 in Kabul, and has "shoulder-length, blond curls" and "thick-lashed turquoise, green eyes" (p. 108). As a child, her father stresses the importance of her education, instilling in her the philosophy that "marriage can wait, education cannot" (p. 114). Yet despite her desire to go to university alongside other forward-thinking women, Afghanistan's society prevents her from doing so. Laila's father takes her out of school because the war has become too dangerous, and after her parents are killed Laila is forced to marry in order to grant her safety within another household. As such, whilst she is an ambitious, proactive individual, the oppressive legislation and war within Afghan society drag her backwards. Yet despite this, Laila continues to fight for her rights by frequently standing up to Rasheed and plotting to escape his household with Aziza and Mariam:

> "She shuddered at what he would do if he found out that she had been stealing from him. Every week, since Aziza's birth, she pried his wallet open when he was asleep or in the outhouse and took a single bill." (p. 241)

By actively defying her husband, Laila stands against the fundamental laws governing Afghan society, risking her own safety and quite possibly her life. Furthermore, even though she is caught when attempting to escape, her stoicism does not waver. For example, when Aziza is sent to an orphanage because Rasheed cannot afford to care for her, she repeatedly ventures out alone to go and see her, despite the fact that women are not allowed to walk the streets without a man. Hosseini writes, "sometimes she was caught, questioned, scolded – two, three, even four times in a single day" but she still "refused to cave in" (p. 313), thus displaying a remarkable strength of will. Furthermore, even when Laila, Tariq, Aziza and Zalmai find safety in Murree in the final part of the novel, Laila "wants to return to Kabul, for Mammy and Babi, for them to see it through *her* eyes" (p. 378). Although she questions whether "they are being foolish [...] leaving behind the safety of Murree" (p. 380), the pull to Kabul is much greater in comparison. Remembering her father's words, "Afghanistan is going to need you" (p. 378), Laila and her family return to Kabul to help rebuild their home. As Laila's endurance and clarity of purpose drives her and her family's life forward, she very much lives up to her childhood nickname, "Laila, Revolutionary Girl" (p. 112).

RASHEED

Rasheed is the husband of both Mariam and Laila. We first meet Rasheed when he is "forty-five at most" (p. 47), and Hosseini offers a very detailed description of his appearance. However, we are first told that Mariam "smelled him before she saw him" (p. 51) due to the pungent smell of "cigarette smoke and thick, sweet cologne" (pp. 51-52). He has a "big, square, ruddy face" with a "hooked nose", "watery, bloodshot eyes", "crowded teeth" and an "impossibly low hairline" (p. 53). Hosseini's description of Rasheed's nails, "yellow-brown, like the inside of a rotting apple" (*ibid.*), significantly seems to mirror the rotten core of his personality. He is violent, manipulative and controlling, subjecting Mariam and Laila to years of domestic abuse and valuing them only as machines designed to produce a male child. He frequently abuses both women in a "systematic business of beating and being beaten, the *thump, thump* of something solid repeatedly striking flesh" (p. 262). Furthermore, Hosseini undercuts all of his redeeming features. For example, Rasheed's parental love for Zalmai is tainted by our awareness of the fact could not love a female child in the same way; meanwhile, on the day of his first son's death Rasheed was supposedly "crying drunk", and had passed out by the time his son "went into the water unnoticed" (pp. 221-222). We therefore see that Rasheed cannot even love his own children responsibly and unconditionally, meaning that it is very difficult to feel any sympathy for him.

ANALYSIS

VIOLENCE

There are two types of violence in the novel, namely domestic violence and political warfare, but the two are inextricably linked. Rasheed's abuse of his wives is driven by the misogyny latent within Afghanistan's societal structures, whereby he subscribes to pre-Taliban and Taliban legislation that destroys women's rights. One of the most horrific moments of domestic violence in the novel occurs when Rasheed attempts to kill Laila after her meeting with Tariq:

> "There was blood on Laila's hands, blood flowing from the open gash on Rasheed's cheek, blood down his neck, on his shirt. He turned around, all snarling teeth and blazing eyes. [...] He was still on top of Laila, his eyes wide and crazy, his hands wrapped around her neck. Laila's face was turning blue now, and her eyes had rolled back. Mariam saw that she was no longer struggling." (p. 339)

Hosseini's vivid description of Laila and Rasheed's bloody injuries creates a very grotesque image, whilst the portrayal of Laila's strangulation is incredibly chilling. Furthermore, Hosseini portrays Rasheed in an animalistic manner using the description "snarling teeth and blazing eyes". Returning to his eyes once again, but this time describing them as "wild and crazy", Hosseini gives the impression that Rasheed is in an uncontrollable, psychopathic-like state. This description of Rasheed's domestic violence, amongst others in the novel, is in part linked with his politics, and more specifically, his sense of superiority to women and desire to control Laila and Mariam. When Laila questions the Taliban's legislation to "make half the population stay at home and do nothing", Rasheed comes back with "why not?" (p. 271).

Meanwhile, such domestic violence is framed against a backdrop of political warfare. Throughout the novel, Hosseini frequently describes the extent of the danger posed to innocent civilians. For example, Laila's childhood friend Giti is killed by a "stray rocket" (p. 175), and Hosseini gives the reader a heartbreaking yet gruesome image of Giti's mother, who "had run up and down the street where Giti was killed, collecting pieces of her daughter's flesh in an apron" (*ibid.*). Hosseini's portrayal of the rocket that kills Laila's family is similarly brutal:

> "Something hot and powerful slammed into her from behind. It knocked her out of her sandals. Lifted her up. And now she was flying, twisting and rotating in the air, seeing sky, then earth, then sky, then earth. A big burning chunk of wood whipped by." (p. 188)

The force with which Laila is struck is apparent within the phrase "seeing sky, then earth, then sky, then earth", which syntactically mirrors the way in which she is spun through the air. Meanwhile, the reader can infer the extent of the damage through the image of a "big burning chunk of wood" that is similarly propelled into the air. The fact that it "hurts [Laila] to breathe" (p. 189) subsequently makes clear the extent of her injuries, and also makes the reader acutely aware of the damage the war has on civilian lives.

THE PLACE OF WOMEN

From the start of the novel, Hosseini shows that women are forced to live under a repressive regime within Afghan society. Mariam's mother tells her that "like a compass needle that points north, a man's accusing finger always finds a woman" (p. 7), a statement that introduces the reader to the fact that men have the ability to blame and shame. Unsurprisingly, such an "accusing finger" manifests within the novel. Whilst Jalil escapes the embarrassment of Mariam's illegitimacy by saying that Nana "forced [herself] on him" (*ibid.*), Rasheed blames Mariam for everything that is wrong with their marriage and in his life. Thus, Nana's message that "there is only one, only one skill a woman like you and me needs in life", to "*tahamul.* Endure" (p. 18) strikes the reader as a damning reflection on the impossible condition that women face. Meanwhile, however, Hosseini also introduces both Mariam and the reader to "modern Afghan women married to modern Afghan men" (p. 74):

> "These women were all swinging handbags and rustling skirts. Mariam even spotted one smoking behind the wheel of a car. Their nails were long, polished pink or orange, their lips red as tulips. They walked in high heels, and quickly, as if on perpetually urgent business." (*ibid.*)

Hosseini's emphasis of the appearance of these modern women signifies how they have control over the way they present themselves; meanwhile, the fact that they are smoking demonstrates that they are privileged with the independence of choosing their own luxuries. Mariam also imagines "that they all had university degrees, that they worked in office buildings, behind desks of their own" (*ibid.*), emphasising their ability to educate themselves and work independently. As such, at this stage in the novel, Hosseini suggests that there is a degree of hope for women, as reflected by these "modern" individuals (*ibid.*).

Yet Hosseini makes it clear that such hope is crushed during the Civil War and the rise of the Taliban in 1996, as they implemented legislation to "make half the population stay at home and do nothing" (p. 271). Claiming "it is not proper for women to wander aimlessly about the streets" (*ibid.*), the Taliban put women in a state of house arrest. They are not even allowed to "laugh in public" or "show [their] face[s]" when outside, and are also "forbidden from attending school" or "working" (*ibid.*). Under the Taliban's regime, women are forced to endure a life virtually devoid of all human rights. However, by the end of the novel Hosseini suggests that the process of rebuilding Afghanistan in the post-Taliban period relies as much on women as it does on men, as Laila reflects on her father's words, *"when this war is over, Afghanistan is going to need you"* (p. 378). Hosseini therefore concludes with a sense of hope regarding the life of women in Afghan society.

HISTORICAL FICTION

A Thousand Splendid Suns is a piece of historical fiction, which means that Hosseini constructs a narrative around factual events. Hosseini deals with a 30-year period of Afghan history, beginning with the overthrow of King Zahir Shah and the monarchy in 1973. Afghanistan was then declared a republic and Daoud Khan became president. The reader learns about this through Jalil: "Afghanistan is no longer a monarchy, Mariam. You see, it's a republic now, and Daoud Khan is the president" (p. 23). Yet as Hosseini informs the reader, disillusionment with Khan's presidency had set in by April 1978, when "a man named Mir Akbar Khyber was found murdered" (p. 96) by the government. Khyber was a prominent member of the People's Democratic Party of Afghanistan (PDPA), and the party overthrew Daoud's government in 1978. As Abdul Qader says in the novel, "a new glorious era in the history of our country is afoot. A new Afghanistan is born" (p. 100).

Book two begins in April 1987, and we learn through Laila's lessons that the Soviets invaded Afghanistan in 1979. Fighting the Soviet occupation is the US-backed army of Mujahideen. By April 1988, Babi informs his family and the reader that, "They're leaving. Within nine months, there won't be any more Soviets in Afghanistan", but they leave in place the "puppet president" (p. 151) Mohammad Najibullah. Yet in 1992, "Najibullah surrendered at last" and the "communist regimes [...] were all defeated" (p. 157); as such, the Mujahideen established their own Government. In this new era, "Afghanistan was now called the Islamic State of Afghanistan. An Islamic Jihadi Council, formed in Peshawar by several of the Mujahideen factions, would oversee things for two months, led by Sibghatullah Mojadidi." (p. 162). However, things soon fell into disarray because "the Mujahideen, armed to the teeth but now lacking a common enemy, had found the enemy in each other" (p. 169). As Hosseini outlines, by June 1992, "there was heavy fighting in West Kabul" (p. 173).

In 1994, the Taliban began "making their way towards Kabul, taking cities from the Mujahideen, ending factional war wherever they'd settled" (p. 267), and they seized Kabul in 1996. After years of repression and fear under the Taliban regime, Hosseini takes us through September 2001, as Laila and Tariq switch on the TV and hear about the Afghan-based al-Qaeda suicide bombers who attacked the twin towers of the United States. The US president George W. Bush subsequently declared war on Afghanistan after the Taliban refused to hand over the al-Qaeda leader Osama bin Laden. We learn that by 2002, "the coalition forces have driven the Taliban out of every major city" (p. 337) and a new president named Hamid Karzai is in power. The novel therefore ends in 2003, when the peacekeeping International Security Assistance Force (ISAF) provides security to Afghan citizens whilst they try to rebuild their country. In this way, Hosseini intersperses the narrative of Laila and Mariam with these historical details to create an accurate portrayal of life in Afghanistan between the mid-1970s and 2003.

FURTHER REFLECTION

SOME QUESTIONS TO THINK ABOUT...

- What do you think about Hosseini's presentation of Jalil? Explain your answer.
- How does Hosseini present the passage of time throughout the novel?
- What is the significance of the title? Justify your answer.
- Take a look at the playscript for *A Thousand Splendid Suns*. How does it differ from the novel?
- To what extent is Mariam's mother a sympathetic character?
- Pick out at least two moments of foreshadowing and explain why they are significant.
- How does Hosseini portray the Soviet Union and America in the novel?
- Consider the fact that in 2006, the International Human Rights Commission registered "over 1,650 cases of violence against women" (Abirafeh, 2009: 145). Do you think

this makes the novel's ending seem overly optimistic? Justify your answer.

We want to hear from you!
Leave a comment on your online library
and share your favourite books on social media!

FURTHER READING

REFERENCE EDITION

- Hosseini, K. (2007) *A Thousand Splendid Suns*. London: Bloomsbury.

REFERENCE STUDIES

- Abirafeh, L. (2009) *Gender and International Aid in Afghanistan: The Politics and Effects of Intervention*. North Carolina: McFarland & Company, Inc.
- Memmott, C. (2004) 'Splendid Suns' burns brightly amid suffering. *USA Today*. [Online]. [Accessed 24 October 2018]. Available from: <http://usatoday30.usatoday.com/life/books/news/2007-05-21-thousand-splendid-suns_N.htm?csp=34>

ADAPTATIONS

- Sarma, U.R. (2018) *A Thousand Splendid Suns (Play Script)*. New York: Riverhead Books.

MORE FROM BRIGHTSUMMARIES.COM

- Reading guide – *The Kite Runner* by Khaled Hosseini.

www.brightsummaries.com

Ebook EAN: 9782808014977

Paperback EAN: 9782808014984

Legal Deposit: D/2018/12603/509

Digital conception by Primento, the digital partner of publishers.

Printed in Great Britain
by Amazon

44865253R00037